Summary: A happy thing happened during a sad time in New York City. Construction workers dug up a strange rock in lower Manhattan which turned out to be a prehistoric egg and inside of the egg was a small dinosaur that would fill the city with great joy and strength.

It's a delightful story about the large impact that little things can have and about remaining strong during difficult times.

ISBN 978-1503064522

MANUFACTURED IN USA

First Edition

Spoon Pen Publishing celebrates the First Amendment and encourages the right to read.

*Living in the Modern World*

Book One:

written by Tiberius St. Judge

illustrated by Ariane Elsammak

SPOON
PEN
PUBLISHING

Spoon Pen Publishing, New York

To the People and
City of New York

The City that Never Sleeps was tired and cranky from struggling all the time. The people of New York City lacked hope. But one bright summer day, a very happy thing happened.

While digging in Battery Park, construction workers came across a strange rock.

The construction workers called their boss. He didn't know what kind of rock it was, either. So, he took out his cellphone and took three pictures of the strange rock.

CLICKETY-CLACK    CLICKETY-CLACK    CLICKETY-CLACK

He sent the pictures to a "Geologist, " a person who studies rocks. His name was Mr. Darwinstein.

Mr. Darwinstein immediately knew what it was.

"It's amber!" he said excitedly.

He wanted a tiny piece of amber to study, so he traveled to Battery Park, put on his safety goggles, and took a chisel from his tool belt. Then he took out his hammer and hit the top of the chisel.

THWACK!

But the amber wasn't solid, and the top cracked, then crumbled to the ground like an old cookie. Mr. Darwinstein was surprised, but he was even more surprised at what was inside the amber.

It was a prehistoric egg that looked like a ......

... Giant Watermelon!

Mr. Darwinstein knew that he needed to contact someone who would know what to do with the egg, just like the construction workers had done when they'd called him. He took out his cellphone and took three pictures.

CLICKETY-CLACK    CLICKETY-CLACK
CLICKETY-CLACK

Mr. Darwinstein sent the pictures to his wife,
Dr. Darwinstein, who rushed right over.

Dr. Darwinstein was a "Paleontologist," someone who studies prehistoric life, like the long ago time of the dinosaurs.

When Dr. Darwinstein saw the large egg, her eyes grew wide with excitement. She touched the egg very gently, then took out a soft brush from her tool belt and brushed off the amber dust. Afterward, she took out a magnifying glass and examined the egg.

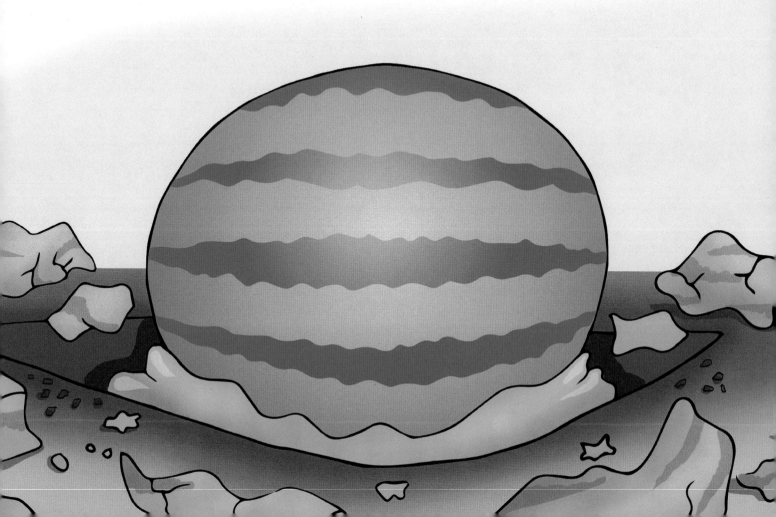

She pressed her left ear to the egg, as if listening for movement inside. But everyone knew that whatever was inside the egg was millions of years old. It couldn't possibly be alive!?

But you know what? Everybody was wrong!

Soon after, everyone heard SCRATCH, SCRATCH, SCRATCH coming from inside the egg. Dr. Darwinstein pulled her head back with a big smile.

A few seconds later - CRACK, CRACK, CRACK! - the top of the egg broke open.

First, the tip of a tail with five small feathers, like little fingers, punched a hole through the top.  Then, it quickly disappeared into the egg again.

Second, a little hand with three stubby, little fingers pulled at the edge of the hole, trying to make it bigger. Then, it , too, disappeared down into the egg.

Third, a stubby face with a tiny nose pushed out of the hole, making the opening even bigger. But the face didn't disappear. It stayed there, blinking at Dr. Darwinstein.

Dr. Darwinstein gasped. She knew the little face was stuck in the hole!

She took out a pair of tongs with soft, red tips from her tool belt and carefully picked off pieces of the shell.

And you know what? It worked , because sometimes a LITTLE help can have a really LARGE impact.

The face pulled back into the egg. But then, with a mighty PUSH, the baby RAMMED the top of it's head through the hole in the egg.

Now, the egg had no top and everyone could see inside, but more importantly, the baby was free to come out.

"It's okay, don't be afraid," Dr. Darwinstein said with her soft voice. "You can come out now."

Soon, two small hands with stubby fingers reached up and grabbed the rim of the shell. Then, a little head slowly rose up out of the egg. The baby started blinking a lot, as if something was caught in its eyes, and then dropped back down into the egg again.

Dr. Darwinstein knew the sun was hurting the baby's eyes, so she moved closer and blocked the sunlight.

And you know what?  It worked.

The baby's little head slowly rose up from inside the egg.  It stared lovingly at Dr. Darwinstein with its big eyes, as if she were its mother.

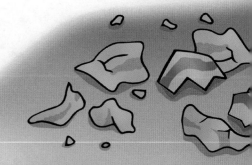

Dr. Darwinstein reached down and carefully picked up the baby. "It's a girl!" Dr. Darwinstein shouted. "But what kind of creature are you?" she asked curiously.

She held the baby up so that everyone could see exactly what it looked like.

The baby looked like a DINOSAUR. But you know what else? It also looked like another animal, too. She looked like a BIRD.

The baby had a stubby face, big blue eyes, and greenish-blue skin, with sprinklings of white spots across the top of its arms, tail, and back, like a dinosaur. But it also had feathers running down the center or its head, across the bottom of the forearms, and at the tip of its tail, like a bird.

So the baby was two things - she was half-dinosaur and half-bird, and that made her even more special.  Everybody stared at her with surprise, because no one had ever seen a FEATHERED-DINOSAUR baby before.

Dr. Darwinstein cradled the little dinosaur in her arms, like she was her own baby. The baby reached up and started playing with Dr. Darwinstein's hair, because it was yellow just like her own feathers.

News about the new feathered-dinosaur baby spread quickly and soon a large crowd gathered at Battery Park. They surrounded Dr. Darwinstein and the new, blue baby, and took a lot of pictures.

Then, they started asking Dr. Darwinstein questions.
"How is it possible that she's alive?" the mayor asked.

"I don't know how she survived being buried all this time, sir."
Dr. Darwinstein replied.
"I guess she's just really, really strong...a real New Yorker."

"Maybe we should rename Battery Park 'Jurassic Park,'
since it's now the birthplace of a dinosaur baby,"
a reporter said jokingly.

"What are we gonna call her?" a little girl asked shyly.

"I'm thinking of naming her 'Julie,' because it's July."
Dr. Darwinstein replied.

"Can we call her 'Jurassic Julie'?"
a little boy asked.

"I don't see why not."
Dr. Darwinstein said.

Everyone nodded in agreement. They loved the name, too. They repeated
"JURASSIC JULIE" out loud, as if they were naming the blue baby themselves.

But you know what else? That wasn't the only reason why the people were cheering.
The people of New York City were happy because little Jurassic Julie had given them
a lot of hope.

They thought that if she could be strong and survive for millions of years while stuck
in an egg, they could be strong and survive anything, too. They could make their
city a happy place again.

The people were happy that Jurassic Julie was born in their city. And you know what else?

Jurassic Julie was happy to be born in New York City, too - her new HOME.

The End

Jurassic Julie goes home with the Darwinsteins, but it can be scary for a little feathered-dinosaur in a new place with new faces. How will she handle it?

To be continued in **Book Two:** "Family"

Made in the USA
Middletown, DE
08 November 2020